Chuck's Truck

by Peggy Perry Anderson

— Green Light Readers —

Houghton Mifflin Harcourt

Boston   New York

This book is dedicated to my Uncle Charley,
"Chuck," who also had an old blue truck.

The Library of Congress has cataloged the hardcover edition
as follows:
Anderson, Peggy Perry.
Chuck's truck/by Peggy Perry Anderson.
p. cm.
"Walter Lorraine books."
Summary: When too many barnyard friends climb in to go to town,
Chuck's truck breaks down, but Handyman Hugh knows
just what to do.
[1. Trucks—Fiction. 2. Domestic animals—Fiction.
3. Stories in rhyme.] I. Title.
2005020870
PZ8.3.A5484Chu 2006
[E]—dc22

ISBN: 978-0-618-66836-6 hardcover
ISBN: 978-0-544-92618-9 paper over board
ISBN: 978-0-544-92619-6 paperback

Manufactured in China
SCP 10 9 8 7 6 5 4 3 2 1
4500647669

This is Chuck.

Chuck goes in his truck.

So does Duck Luck

5

and the chicken. "Cluck! Cluck!"

Now Nip and Tuck ride in the truck.

Up, up, up jumps the burro Buck!

Huck the horse and Fat Cat Pat go too.

Don't forget Sue and Lou!

Oh! Oh! Oh! Flo wants to go.
And so . . .

15

when they
get to town

17

the truck

BOOM!

breaks

POW!

down!

Old Blue is through!

This is bad.

Chuck is very,
very sad.
The animals try
to make him glad.

"We can come,"
says Handy Hugh.

His crew always knows

just what to do.

Together they make the truck like new.

Here is Chuck.

Here is Chuck's truck,

all ready to go to town.

This time Chuck's truck will
NOT
break down!